The Case Of The 2O² Clues ™

The New Adventures of MARY-KATE & ASHLEY ™

The Case Of The 2Ö² Clues ™

by Nina Alexander

DUALSTAR PUBLICATIONS ™ PARACHUTE PRESS

SCHOLASTIC INC.

New York   Toronto   London   Auckland   Sydney

DUALSTAR PUBLICATIONS PARACHUTE PRESS

Dualstar Publications
c/o Thorne and Company
1801 Century Park East
Los Angeles, CA 90067

Parachute Press
156 Fifth Avenue
Suite 325
New York, NY 10010

Published by Scholastic Inc.

With special thanks to Robert Thorne and Harold Weitzberg.

Printed in the U.S.A.
February 1998
ISBN: 0-590-29307-9
A B C D E F G H I J

THE WORLD'S BEST PET

"**W**here's my other purple sneaker?" I cried. "I can't go to the adopt-a-pet show at the mall with only one shoe!"

"Why don't you let Clue find it for you, Mary-Kate?" Ashley asked. She pulled her strawberry blond hair into a ponytail. "Finding things is what she does best."

It's true. Clue is our basset hound. And she is amazing at finding things.

That makes her the perfect dog for Ashley and me, because we're detectives. We run the

Olsen and Olsen Mystery Agency out of the attic of our house.

We call Clue our silent partner. Clue's nose has helped us sniff out a lot of clues in a lot of cases.

But right now I needed Clue to help me find a shoe, not a clue.

I sat down on my bed next to Clue. She was in the middle of her morning nap.

I woke her up and let her smell my foot. "Find my sneaker, Clue," I said.

Clue jumped down off the bed. She ran to the closet and nosed it open. She dug under a pile of clean clothes and pulled out something purple.

"My sneaker!" I cried. "Good girl, Clue. You're the smartest dog ever!"

"I told you she would find it," Ashley said. "You would have thought of asking Clue for help yourself if you just took the time to stop and think," she added.

Ashley loves to stop and think. I usually

jump right into things.

People expect us to act alike because we look alike. But we don't act alike at all. In fact, we're completely different from each other.

"Ashley! Mary-Kate! Your friends are here!" Mom called from downstairs.

I grabbed my backpack and stuck my mini tape recorder inside. I use the recorder to make notes whenever Ashley and I are on a case. I take it everywhere—because you never know when or where a mystery will turn up.

Ashley and I raced down the stairs. Clue ran after us. Her long ears flopped up and down with every step.

Samantha Samuels and Tim Park waited for us at the bottom of the staircase. Samantha, Tim, Ashley, and I are all in the same fourth-grade class. We hang out together all the time.

"Guess what?" Samantha exclaimed. She bounced up and down on her toes. Her curly red hair flew around her face. Her brown eyes sparkled. "Tim's parents said he could actually adopt a pet today at the mall."

"That's so great!" I cried. "What are you going to get?"

Tim didn't answer right away. That's because his mouth was full, as usual. Tim is the tallest and skinniest kid in our class. And he's always eating something. Today he had half of a banana in his hand. The other half was in his mouth.

He gave a big gulp. "I haven't decided what kind of pet I want yet," he said. "My mom told me I could get whatever I wanted—as long as it would never weigh more than sixty pounds."

"You're going to have a lot to choose from," Samantha said. She pulled a folded piece of newspaper out of her pocket. She smoothed it out and pointed to the ad for the adopt-a-pet show.

"It says there are going to be kittens, and puppies, and birds, and turtles, and snakes, and hamsters. Every kind of pet you can think of—and tons of them won't grow too big," Samantha told us. She started to fold the newspaper back up.

"Hey, wait! Let me see that," I said. Samantha handed me the paper, and I quickly unfolded it.

"I saw something about a basset hound," I told them. "I love to read about my favorite kind of dog." I studied the paper.

Ashley peered over my shoulder. She pointed to the bottom of the page. "There it is—an article about a basset hound who disappeared," she said.

I quickly read the story. "The dog's name is Spanish Sweetheart—Sweetie for short," I said. "She's a famous show dog. They call her the million-dollar dog because she's won so many dog shows."

Tim crowded in next to me and studied the article. "It says Sweetie was supposed to be in a big dog show tomorrow," he told us.

"That's very interesting. Does it say where

Sweetie disappeared?" Ashley asked.

Ashley likes to get all the facts. That's one of the things that makes her such a good detective.

"She was last seen on Daisy Drive," I answered. "That's near the fairgrounds."

"Yes," I told her. "It says here that Sweetie's owner sent her daughter to drive Sweetie to the fairgrounds. That's where the dog show is going to be."

Ashley read over my shoulder. "It also says that Sweetie was lost when the daughter stopped and got out of the car to ask for directions," she added.

"Right." I said. "She set Sweetie's carrier on the ground so Sweetie could get some air. But when she came back to the car the carrier was empty. And Sweetie had disappeared!"

"Sweetie's owner must feel terrible," Samantha said. "I wouldn't be able to stand it if Sparky got lost."

Sparky is Samantha's basset hound. He's

Clue's best friend. Samantha only lives around the block, so Sparky and Clue get to play with each other all the time.

Ashley bent down and gave Clue a big hug. I knew she was thinking how much we would miss Clue if *Clue* ever disappeared.

Tim stuffed the rest of his banana in his mouth. "I hope they find Sweetie soon," he mumbled.

"They should. Sweetie's owner hired a private detective," I said. "And they're giving a big reward to the person who finds her."

Ashley read over my shoulder. "Sweetie has a heart-shaped birthmark. That's where the 'Sweetheart' part of her name comes from. And she only understands Spanish. So that explains the 'Spanish' part."

Tim pushed his long black hair out of his eyes. "A dog who understands Spanish," he said. "That's pretty cool. Maybe I'll get a dog. I could ask my grandmother to teach it Korean."

Tim's grandmother was born in Korea. She

speaks English and Korean. She's trying to teach Tim to speak Korean. But he only knows a few words so far.

"You'd better get her to teach you some more Korean, too," Samantha teased. "Otherwise your dog won't understand anything you say."

Our little sister Lizzie burst through the kitchen door and ran over to us. "Mom says to remember to walk Clue before you go."

"But we have to leave now or all the good pets will be gone before we get there," I said. "Tim is going to end up with a goldfish or something."

"I have a plan," Ashley said. "We'll get Trent to trade turns with us. I'll go ask him to walk Clue." She dashed up the stairs.

Ashley is the best at coming up with plans. I'm glad *one* of us is!

A few moments later Ashley ran back down the stairs with a big smile on her face.

"He'll do it," she told us. "But he made me

make a deal with him. We have to walk Clue for him twice. And we have to bring him a cookie from the mall."

"That figures," I mumbled. Our big brother Trent won't do *anything* unless you make a deal with him.

"Let's get out of here before he decides he wants *two* cookies," I said. "We have to get to the mall so we can find Tim the best pet in the adopt-a-pet show!"

Ashley grinned. "You mean, the best pet in the world!'

2

TWO MISSING PUPPIES

"**L**et's go to the mall information booth and ask where the animals are," Ashley said.

"We don't need to do that," I told her. "All we have to do is follow our ears." I headed in the direction of the squeaks, squawks, meows, and barks.

We turned the corner. "Oh, wow," Samantha murmured.

Rows and rows of cages and tanks were arranged around the big fountain in the center of the mall. We ran toward them.

I tried to look at everything at once. I saw a cat with the longest, whitest, softest-looking fur. And another cat with no hair at all!

Rabbits with their cute little cotton-ball tails hopped around one cage. A snake flicked its pointy black tongue in and out in another. A potbellied pig grunted at me from the last cage in the row.

"Tim, how about that pig?" I asked.

But Tim couldn't stop staring at a huge Great Dane. "Whoa. I don't think that dog would even fit in my house."

"And he definitely weighs more than sixty pounds *now*. Your mom would flip if you brought him home," I added.

"We need a plan so Tim can see every pet they have before he decides," Ashley said. "Let's walk around the fountain clockwise and—"

Samantha grabbed my arm. "Look! They have two basset puppies!"

That made even Ashley forget about her

plan. We dashed over to the bassets' cage. The two puppies were playing tug-of-war with a chew toy.

They were both so cute. One had a big round spot on her forehead. The other had one white ear and one brown ear.

"That one." Tim pointed to the puppy with one white ear and one brown ear. "That's the one I want."

"Are you sure? You haven't looked at all the other animals yet," Ashley said.

"That's the one I want," Tim repeated.

A plump lady strolled over to us. She wore a T-shirt that said, "Man's best friend's best friend—The Eastside Animal Shelter."

"Hi, I'm Mrs. Roberts," she said. "If you're interested in adopting the puppy, you'll have to fill out one of these."

Mrs. Roberts picked up a pad of application forms from the table next to the puppies' cage. She handed it to Tim.

I studied it over his shoulder. There were

spaces for him to fill in his name, address, and phone number, and a list of questions for him to answer.

"How many people live in your house? Do you have any other pets?" Tim read.

"I know it's a lot of questions," Mrs. Roberts said. "But we have to ask them so we can be sure all of our animals will find good homes."

"Can you tell me about that iguana?" a teenage boy asked Mrs. Roberts.

"Sure." Mrs. Roberts turned to Tim. "Give me a yell when you're finished." She hurried over to the iguana cage.

"Mary-Kate! Ashley! Samantha! Tim!" a loud voice called.

"Oh, no," Ashley said. "Is that who I think it is?"

Tim groaned. Even Samantha frowned. And Samantha almost always has a smile on her face. She's the happiest girl I know.

I glanced over my shoulder. "It's her, all right. Princess Patty!"

Patty O'Leary is in our class at school. We call her Princess Patty because her parents buy her everything she wants. And she always wants whatever other kids have.

Patty ran up to us. "What are you doing here?" she demanded.

"Tim is going to adopt one of these puppies," Ashley answered. She always tries to be polite. Even when she's talking to Patty.

I like to be polite, too, but it's hard when Patty is around.

"Maybe I'll adopt one, too," Patty announced. She kneeled down on the floor. She opened the cage and grabbed the puppy with the big spot on her forehead.

"Do you know what bassets like to eat?" Patty asked. "What are their favorite toys? Do they sleep on a blanket or a pillow or in a special bed?"

"You shouldn't adopt a puppy just because Tim is getting one," I said.

Patty glared at me. "Don't tell me what to

do, Mary-Kate," she snapped. "You're not my mother. I don't have to listen to you!"

Patty hugged the puppy too hard. The puppy let out a little squeal and wiggled her legs.

"Stop it," I cried. I reached for the puppy.

I guess I took Patty by surprise. She let go right away.

"You think you're so smart. All of you," Patty yelled. "But you don't know anything!" She tossed her brown ponytail over her shoulder and stormed away.

I put the puppy back in the cage and closed the latch. "Patty is so—oof!"

I said "oof" because someone bumped into me.

I turned around, rubbing my right arm. I saw a tall woman with dark curly hair. "Sorry," the woman said. "I was in such a hurry I didn't see you."

She rushed over to Mrs. Roberts. "Do you have any more bassets?" she demanded.

"Where did these puppies come from?"

"Patty is so—oof!"

I said "oof" again because someone *else* bumped into me.

"Hey," I complained, rubbing my left shoulder. "Am I invisible or something?"

"Are those basset hounds?" the short man who bumped into me asked. He ran his hand through his thinning hair.

He hadn't even apologized for bumping me. But I answered politely. "Yes, they are," I told him. "Aren't they cute?"

He glanced around the mall. He seemed nervous. "Sure, sure," he said.

He grabbed a pad of application forms from the pile on the table and started to fill out the top one. His hand shook a little as he wrote. He pressed down hard with his pen.

The puppy with the spot on her forehead pushed her face against the cage and licked the nervous man's shoe. The man didn't even notice.

I exchanged a glance with Ashley. I could tell we were both thinking the same thing. He wasn't paying any attention to the puppies—so why did he want to adopt one of them?

Samantha must have been thinking that, too. "Are you going to adopt one of the bassets?" she asked the nervous man.

He didn't even look up. "No," he answered. "I'm not going to adopt one puppy. I'm going to adopt both of them."

Tim looked up from his own application. "But I want the one with the white ear," he said.

The curly-haired woman finished talking to Mrs. Roberts and hurried off. Mrs. Roberts made her way over to the nervous man.

"Can I help you?" she asked.

"I want to adopt both of these puppies," he told her.

She shook her head. "I'm sorry," she said. "This young man has already requested one."

The man glared at Tim. He ripped his application form off the pad. "Fine," he said. "In

that case, I've changed my mind." He tore the application form into pieces, tossed it into a wastebasket, and stomped away.

"We'd like to adopt that parrot," a woman with a little girl said.

"I'll be back in a couple of minutes," Mrs. Roberts told us.

Tim filled in the last line of his application. "Done," he said.

"Let's get Trent his cookie while we wait for Mrs. Roberts," Ashley said. "The store is right over there."

"I'll be right back," Tim promised his puppy.

We bought Trent his cookie, and Tim bought himself a cookie. Then we hurried back to the puppies.

Ashley gasped. She pointed to the puppies' cage.

"Oh, no!" I cried. "The cage is empty!"

"The basset puppies are gone!" Ashley exclaimed.

ANOTHER BASSET GONE!

"**S**omeone took my puppy!" Tim yelled. He almost started choking on the cookie in his mouth.

"We were only gone a couple minutes. Did Mrs. Roberts let someone else adopt them?" Samantha asked.

"Come on," I said. "We've got to find her!"

"She's over by the bunny cage," Ashley said. We raced over to Mrs. Roberts.

"What happened to the basset puppies, Mrs. Roberts?" Tim asked. "You didn't let someone adopt mine, did you?"

"Of course not," Mrs. Roberts said. "Your puppy is—" She turned toward the basset puppies' cage. Her eyes widened. Her mouth dropped open. "Gone!" she cried.

"We went to get cookies," Ashley explained. "We were only gone a minute. When we came back the cage door was open—and the puppies had disappeared!"

"I have to report this," Mrs. Roberts said. "I'll be right back."

We wandered over to the empty cage. Tim picked up one of the puppies' toys and gave it a little squeak. He looked really upset.

"Maybe whoever took the puppies is still in the mall," I said. "Let's go look for them."

"Good idea," Ashley said. "Samantha and Tim, why don't you wait for Mrs. Roberts. Mary-Kate and I will search the mall and meet you back here."

Tim nodded. He kept staring sadly at the empty cage.

Ashley and I took off through the mall.

We dashed into the video store. No puppies. We checked the bookstore. No puppies.

We circled the food court. No puppies.

I pulled my mini tape recorder out of my backpack. "This is Mary-Kate Olsen. It is 12:17 P.M. Ashley and I are at work on a mystery in the Meadow Mall. Two basset hound puppies have disappeared." I clicked off the recorder.

"The puppies couldn't have gotten out of the cage by themselves," Ashley said. "Do we have any suspects?"

I glanced into a sporting goods store. No sign of the puppies. But I spotted a whole table full of soccer balls.

"The nervous man!" I blurted out.

The soccer balls reminded me of Trent, and how nervous he was before his big soccer game last week. And thinking about that reminded me of the nervous man who wanted to adopt the puppies.

That's how my mind works. Ashley doesn't

understand it. A lot of people don't.

"The nervous man hardly paid any attention to the puppies," I said. "That was very suspicious, since he said he wanted *both* of them."

Ashley sat down on one of the benches in front of the jewelry store. She pulled out our detective notebook and started to write.

I sighed. I keep trying to convince Ashley to use her mini tape recorder. But she won't. She says writing things down helps her think more clearly.

Great-grandma Olive gave us the tape recorders. She's the best. She's always sending us things to help us in our detective work.

Great-grandma Olive is the reason we became detectives. She loves mysteries so much that we started to love them, too.

"Okay. The nervous man is suspect number one," Ashley said. "But we should try to think of other suspects, too. Just like Great-grandma Olive taught us."

"You're right about that," I said. "Who else

could have done it?"

Ashley bit her lip. "Mrs. Roberts was around the puppies' cages a lot."

I could tell Ashley didn't like the idea that Mrs. Roberts stole the puppies. Mrs. Roberts seemed way too nice to be a dognapper.

But good detectives have to consider every possibility. Ashley and I always try to remember that.

"Why would Mrs. Roberts take the puppies?" I asked. "She doesn't have a motive."

"That's true," Ashley said. "No motive."

Great-grandma Olive taught us that word. A motive is a reason why somebody would want to do something.

"What about that tall woman with the dark curly hair?" Ashley asked. "She was around just before the puppies disappeared."

"And she did ask Mrs. Roberts some questions about the puppies," I said.

Ashley made notes on our suspects in the notebook. I read over her shoulder.

"SUSPECT #1: Nervous man," she wrote. "POSSIBLE MOTIVE: He wanted both puppies but couldn't have them. SUSPECT #2: Mysterious, curly-haired woman. POSSIBLE MOTIVE: Unknown. Very curious about puppies."

"I have another person to add to the list," I said when she was finished. "Patty."

Ashley frowned. "Patty is a pain. But do you really think she would steal the puppies?"

"You know Princess Patty," I said. "She always wants whatever somebody else has. She knew Tim wanted one of the puppies. Maybe she took both of them so Tim couldn't have any."

"There you are!" someone cried.

It was Samantha. She and Tim hurried toward us.

"Mrs. Roberts said we shouldn't keep trying to find the puppies," Tim told us. "She called the police. And she said she'd phone me as soon as she finds out anything."

"I guess we should just go home then," I

said. A little girl wheeled a doll carriage past us. A tiny poodle puppy sat inside.

Tim stared down at the ground. I could tell he was thinking about *his* puppy.

"Could we go get Clue and bring her over to visit Sparky?" Tim asked. "At least then I could play with some bassets."

"Great idea!" Samantha said.

"It always smells so good in your house," Tim told Samantha.

I laughed. Tim thought it smelled good because it smelled like *food*. Samantha's dad always has a yummy cake or a batch of his special walnut chocolate-chip cookies in the oven.

Samantha pulled open the sliding glass doors in the kitchen and led the way into the backyard.

Samantha's dad hurried over. A big smile spread across his face when he saw us. "Great! You have Sparky."

"That's not Sparky, that's Clue," Samantha said.

"You didn't take Sparky with you?" her dad asked. He sounded worried.

"I didn't take him anywhere," Samantha answered. "We just brought Clue over to play with him."

Samantha's dad shook his head. "I'm sorry, sweetheart," he said. "I've been searching for half an hour. I'm afraid Sparky is missing!"

THE SEARCH BEGINS!

"I don't know how it happened," Samantha's dad said. "Sparky was sleeping in the backyard one minute. Then the next minute he was gone!"

"What do you mean, gone?" Samantha said. "He can't be gone! Where would he go?"

"Did you see anyone?" I asked. "Did you hear any strange sounds?"

Samantha's dad shook his head.

Samantha grabbed me by the arm. "You have to help me find him," she begged. Her eyes filled with tears. "We have to find Sparky!"

I put my arm around Samantha's shoulders. "Don't worry," I said. "Olsen and Olsen will find him. I promise."

"Samantha's dad already looked for Sparky. But he may have missed some clues," Ashley said. "Let's each search a different part of the yard."

"What should we look for?" Tim asked.

"Anything can be a clue," I told him. "Just look for things that seem out of place. Maybe someone took Sparky. And maybe whoever took him dropped something that will lead us to Sparky."

"Right. We never know what clues will help us figure out a case," Ashley said. "Mary-Kate, why don't you check Sparky's doghouse while I search the garden?" she asked.

"I'll look around the front yard," Tim offered.

Having a plan seemed to make Samantha

feel a little bit better. "I'll search the house," she said. "I know all Sparky's favorite spots."

I hurried over to Sparky's doghouse. Clue padded along behind me.

I studied the ground for footprints.

I searched for anything that might belong to a dognapper—a button, a piece of cloth, a scrap of paper, anything that could help us find Sparky.

But all I saw was grass and dirt. And more grass and more dirt.

I stuck my head inside the house. But all I found was one of Sparky's squeaky toys and a half-eaten bone.

I heard Samantha and Tim come back into the yard. I turned around. I could tell by their faces that neither of them had found any clues either.

I glanced over at Ashley. She shook her head.

"Sparky is gone for good," Samantha wailed. "Just like Tim's puppy! And we don't

even have one clue!"

Ashley and I rushed over to them. "It's time to bring in the Super-Duper Snooper," Ashley said.

That's what we call Clue's nose—the Super-Duper Snooper. All basset hounds have sensitive noses. But Clue's is awesome.

"You should have seen how fast Clue found my sneaker this morning," I told Samantha and Tim. "She's going to be a big help on this case."

I ran over to Sparky's doghouse and grabbed his squeaky toy. Then I raced back and knelt down in front of Clue. I let her smell the toy.

Ashley kneeled down beside me. "Find Sparky, Clue," she urged. "You can do it. Find Sparky!"

Clue sniffed at the toy. Then she took off.

"All right!" Tim shouted. "Clue's on the trail!"

We ran after her. She kept her nose to the

ground and headed around the side of the house. She stopped at the back gate and gave a high bark.

Ashley opened the gate for her. Clue crossed the front yard—and stopped at the driveway to the house next door.

"It's Patty's house!" I gasped.

Clue took a few more sniffs. She walked around in a little circle.

"What's going on?" Tim asked.

"Maybe it's harder for Clue to sniff out the trail on the driveway than on the grass," Ashley said. "Or maybe someone picked Sparky up and carried him inside."

I held the squeaky toy out in front of Clue's nose. She gave it a sniff.

She made another little circle. Then she sat down in the middle of the driveway and whined sadly.

"The trail definitely ends here," I said. "And that means Patty took Sparky."

"But what is her motive?" Ashley asked.

"We know why she wanted the puppies. But why would she take Sparky?"

"I don't know," I answered. "But I'm going to find out."

5

I GET A HUNCH

I marched up to Patty's front door and rang the doorbell. Ashley, Tim, and Samantha followed me.

"I don't think this is a good idea," Ashley whispered. "You're rushing into things, Mary-Kate. We need a lot more clues before we know who took Sparky or the puppies."

"Clue led us straight to Patty's driveway. That's a good enough clue for me." I rang the bell again.

I didn't hear anyone moving around inside

the house. I didn't see any lights on. "I guess nobody's home," I said.

"What do we do now?" Tim asked.

"Let's get Clue to try one more time," I suggested.

Samantha nodded. "Maybe she was just tired or something."

I hurried back over to Clue. I knelt down next to her and held Sparky's squeaky toy in front of her nose. "Come on, girl. Use that Super-Duper Snooper."

But Clue just whined and rested her head on her paws.

"What's wrong with her?" Tim asked.

I had a hunch I knew the answer. "She must be upset about Sparky's disappearance," I said. "Sparky is her best friend."

I tugged gently at Clue's collar. But Clue didn't budge.

Samantha bent down to pat her. "Poor Clue," she said. "She looks almost as sad as I feel. We both miss Sparky already."

I scratched Clue's head. "I guess we'd better take her home. Then we can decide what to do next about finding Sparky."

"Do you want me to come with you?" Samantha asked.

Ashley shook her head. "I think it's a better plan for you to stay here," she said. "Call us if Sparky comes back."

"I'll stay here, too," Tim told us. "I can keep Samantha company."

"Come on, Clue," I said. I picked her up. She's always heavy. But for some reason, she seemed even heavier when she was sad. I grunted with the effort as I carried her over to our bikes.

I set her down in Ashley's bike basket. Then I glanced over at Patty's house. I still thought she might be the one who took the dogs.

"Don't worry, Samantha," Ashley said as she put up the kickstand on her bike. "We'll find Sparky."

"We'll find your puppy, too, Tim," I

promised. "Olsen and Olsen cracks every case."

"Thanks," Samantha and Tim said at the same time. They waved as Ashley and I rode off toward our house.

As I pedaled, I kept glancing over at Clue. Usually she loves bike rides. But she still looked really sad.

We parked our bikes in front of the garage. I helped Clue out of Ashley's basket and set her down in our front yard. She headed over to her favorite spot under the big pine tree near the porch.

"Hey," a voice yelled. "Girls! I need to talk to you."

We turned around, and I saw a woman climb out of a green mini van. A woman with dark, curly hair. "It's that woman from the mall!" I whispered. "Suspect number two."

I knew we shouldn't be talking to strangers. But we might get some important clues from the curly-haired woman.

I glanced back at the house. Ashley and I could run to our front door in about two seconds if we had to.

The woman took a few steps up our driveway and pointed to Clue. "Is that your basset?" she asked. "I'd like to see her up close, if you don't mind."

Ashley frowned. "What do you want with our dog?" she asked.

The woman kept staring at Clue. "I just want to see her for a second," she answered.

Ashley leaned toward me. "Why would she want to see Clue?" she whispered.

"I don't know," I whispered back. "Unless she's the dognapper! Maybe she's planning to grab Clue and drive away."

Clue sighed and stood up. She wandered toward us.

I didn't want her going anywhere near that woman. "Clue—sit!" I ordered.

Clue is very well trained, even when she's sad. She sat down right away.

The woman spun around and raced back to the green van. She jumped inside and took off down the street.

"That was weird," Ashley said.

"Yeah," I agreed. "She seemed so interested in seeing Clue up close. Then she just drove off."

I clicked on my tape recorder. I needed to add to my notes on the case.

"It's 3:42 P.M. Our case is getting stranger and stranger," I said into the recorder. "Another basset hound disappeared—Sparky Samuels. That makes three basset hounds who have dis—"

"Not three. Four!" Ashley exclaimed. "We forgot about Spanish Sweetie. She disappeared, too, remember?"

"Hey, that's right. And I just got one of my hunches," I told Ashley. "Come on!"

6

OUR BRILLIANT TRICK

"**I** wish *I* got a hunch once in a while," Ashley complained.

I took the attic steps two at a time. "You make plans. I get hunches. That's what makes us a great team," I answered.

I burst into our detective office and hurried straight to our metal filing cabinet. I jerked open the middle drawer.

Ashley and I keep files on all kinds of subjects—poisonous plants, skydiving, kangaroos. Anything and everything that we might be able to use in one of our cases.

I pulled out the membership list of the Basset Lovers Club of California. It has the names and phone numbers of tons of people who own bassets.

"I want to call some of the other basset owners in town," I told Ashley. I picked up my pink phone and started to dial.

"Why?" Ashley asked.

"Because maybe *more* than four bassets have disappeared," I answered. "Shh. It's ringing."

A man answered. He sounded upset.

"Hi, I'm Mary-Kate Olsen," I said. "I'm calling about your basset hound. I—"

"You found Howler! Is he okay? I've been so worried about him," the man cried.

"No, no. I'm sorry. I didn't find your dog," I said. "I was calling because some other basset hounds have disappeared."

"Oh," he muttered.

He sounded so disappointed. "Don't worry,"

I told him. "The Olsen and Olsen detective team is on the case. We're going to find all the missing bassets—including Howler."

I gave him our phone number so he could call us if he found Howler. And I told him we would call as soon as we knew anything.

When I hung up, Ashley dialed her blue phone. She looked upset as she began talking.

"Okay, Mrs. Linden," she said. "I promise we'll call you." Ashley hung up.

"Disappeared?" I asked. Ashley nodded.

"Now we have *six* missing bassets." This case was getting bigger by the second.

"We need a plan," Ashley said. "Let's give this list to Samantha and Tim. They can call every basset owner in town and find out if there are more missing dogs."

"Okay. But what are *we* going to do?" I asked.

"We have to return to the scene of the crime," Ashley said. "We have to go to the mall!"

Ashley and I hurried into the mall. I held Clue's leash tightly.

Ashley and I wanted to keep Clue with us every second. We didn't want Clue to disappear, too! Lucky for us, dogs were allowed in the mall today because of the adopt-a-pet show.

"I'm still not sure what we're doing here," I said. "We already checked every store."

"But we were looking for puppies—not clues," Ashley answered. "Let's start back by the basset puppies' cage."

We rushed over to the cage—and found Mrs. Roberts standing at the table beside it.

"Have the police found out anything about the missing puppies?" Ashley asked her.

Mrs. Roberts shook her head. "No. But they promised to keep looking."

"Have you noticed anything suspicious around here?" I asked. "Any strange people hanging around?"

"No, everyone who has stopped by has

been very nice." Mrs. Roberts straightened a stack of application pads and sighed.

"Oh, that reminds me," she said. "A friend of yours came by a few times to ask about basset hounds."

"A friend of ours?" Ashley said in surprise. "Who was it?"

"She didn't tell me her name," Mrs. Roberts said. "But she was about your age, with a brown ponytail. She said she knew you."

Ashley and I glanced at each other. We were both thinking the same thing. Patty!

"Excuse me," a teenage girl called to Mrs. Roberts. "Is it true you can train a rabbit to use a litter box?"

"Yes, it is," Mrs. Roberts answered. She waved good-bye to Ashley and me and headed toward the rabbit cage.

"So Patty has been hanging around the basset table," I said. "That makes her look very guilty."

"I don't think so," Ashley said. "I think it

gives her an alibi."

Alibi is another word we learned from Great-grandma Olive. An alibi is a reason why a person could not have committed a crime.

"Patty couldn't have been dognapping Sparky—because she was here talking to Mrs. Roberts," Ashley said. "And she didn't have the missing puppies from the mall with her, either."

"I guess Patty didn't take the puppies or Sparky," I said. "Now we're down to two suspects: the curly-haired woman and the nervous man."

"We did see the curly-haired woman at our house. That means she was in the neighborhood around the time Sparky was stolen," Ashley said.

"Yeah. And Sweetie was stolen from our neighborhood, too!" I added. "I bet the curly-haired woman is the dognapper."

"But what about the nervous man?" Ashley asked. "We can't forget about him." She flipped open her notebook and began to write.

"I wish the nervous man had turned in his application," I said. "Then we would know how to find him."

"He didn't hand in a form," Ashley said slowly. "But he did fill one out."

I shrugged. "So what?" I said. "He ripped it up into tiny pieces and threw it away."

I peeked into the trash can. "And someone already emptied the trash. So we can't even try to piece it back together."

"I know," Ashley said. "But there still might be a way to get the clue we need."

She grinned at me. "Remember the pencil trick Great-grandma Olive taught us?"

"Oh, yeah! Ashley, you're brilliant!" I exclaimed. "I just hope the trick works!"

7

DEAD END!

I pulled a pencil out of my backpack and handed it to Ashley.

She grabbed one of the application pads. She turned the pencil sideways and rubbed the edge of the pencil lead across the paper.

"Most people press down hard when they write." Ashley continued to shade the paper. I watched as she moved the pencil across the top application form.

The pencil colored the paper—except for the part where someone had pressed down to write on the form above it. Soon words appeared, like white shadows in the black lead.

The trick worked! Great-grandma Olive's trick worked! We found the hidden message!

I bent over and studied the paper. "That's not it," I said. "It's Tim's! I can read his name in the shaded area."

Ashley grabbed another pad and started rubbing the pencil lead across the top sheet. This time the name that appeared wasn't familiar.

"Larry Katz," I read. I looked at my sister. "Do you think that's the nervous man?"

"I'm sure of it." Ashley pointed to the bottom of the application. Larry Katz hadn't finished filling out all of the spaces.

"See?" Ashley said. "He stopped in the middle and ripped it off the pad, remember?" She copied Larry Katz's address into her notebook.

"Treadmill Lane," I said. "I know where that is. We went to a birthday party there once.

Don't you remember?"

Ashley looked confused. "We did?"

I nodded. "Don't worry, just follow me!"

We raced out to our bikes. I carried Clue. She has such short legs that she can't run very fast.

"It's only about three blocks from here," I yelled as we rode off.

I made a right turn, then a left turn, then another left turn. "Here it is." I pointed to the Treadmill Lane street sign.

"Now we have to find 787," Ashley said.

The address of the closest house was 117 Treadmill Lane. The next house was 119. The next house was 121.

"Oh, no!" I gasped.

Treadmill Lane was a dead end. And 121 was the last house on the street. The numbers didn't go any higher.

There was no 787 Treadmill Lane!

Ashley and I stopped our bikes and stared at each other.

"Maybe there is *another* Treadmill Lane," Ashley said. But she didn't sound very hopeful.

Clue gave a little bark. Then she leaped out of my bike basket and raced down the sidewalk.

"Clue!" I shouted. "Come back!"

Ashley and I dropped our bikes and ran after Clue. She cut through a flower garden.

I leaped over a rose bush and tackled her.

"Let her go," Ashley said.

"Why?" I asked.

"Don't you hear it?" she asked. "Listen."

Then I heard it, too. Barking dogs. A bunch of them.

"The missing dogs!" I cried.

"Maybe," Ashley agreed. "And Clue is going to lead us to them."

I let Clue go. She shoved her way through a low hedge. Ashley and I grabbed our bikes and wheeled them down the sidewalk after Clue.

Clue loped across to the end of the block and turned the corner. She raced across the

lawn of a yellow house.

Then she slid to a stop in front of the wooden fence leading to the backyard.

Clue gave a loud bark. A lot of answering barks came from behind the fence.

We dropped our bikes in the driveway and rushed over to the fence. "Quick. Let's see if they're the missing bassets!" I exclaimed.

Ashley knelt down and cupped her hands. "I'll give you a boost."

I stuck my foot in Ashley's hands and she shoved me up toward the top of the fence.

"I can't see," I called down to Ashley.

She gave a little grunt and boosted me higher into the air. "Bassets!" I exclaimed. "I see bassets!"

"Hey!" someone yelled. "Get away from those dogs!"

8

WITHOUT A CLUE!

Ashley and I whirled around. A short woman with white hair rushed over to us.

"You're upsetting the puppies," she scolded.

"We just wanted to look at them," Ashley told her. "I'm Ashley Olsen. And this is my sister, Mary-Kate. We're trying to find six missing basset hounds."

"Someone has been dognapping bassets all over town," I added.

"Oh, that's terrible," the woman cried. "I'm Mrs. Nelson. I'm sorry I yelled at you. I just got worried when I heard the puppies barking like that."

"That's okay," Ashley told her.

"The puppies are presents for my grandchildren," Mrs. Nelson told us. "Would you like to see them?"

"Yes!" I exclaimed. I wanted to get a better look at the bassets.

Mrs. Nelson led us around the side of the house and swung open a gate.

Six roly-poly puppies ran up to us. One puppy grabbed my shoelace and started to chew. Another puppy jumped up and licked Clue on the nose.

"I don't see a puppy with one white ear and one brown ear," Ashley whispered to me. "Or a puppy with a spot on its forehead."

I quickly studied the puppies. Ashley was right. The two puppies from the adopt-a-pet show weren't here.

And neither was Sparky, Sweetie, or the other two bassets. Those dogs were all adults, not little puppies, like these dogs.

"Thanks for letting us see the puppies," Ashley said. "You should be extra careful with them until we catch the dognapper."

"I will," Mrs. Nelson said. "Good luck."

Ashley started for the gate. Then she stopped and turned around.

"Do you know if there is another Treadmill Lane anywhere in town?" she asked. "We think one of our suspects lives at 787 Treadmill Lane. But there is no 787 on this street."

"Another Treadmill Lane?" Mrs. Nelson said. "I don't think so. But I have a map in the house. Let's go check."

Ashley and I followed Mrs. Nelson to the back door. She waved to the puppies. "Adios!" she called to them.

"I like to speak Spanish to them," she told us. She led the way inside. "Their mother is a famous show dog from Spain."

"Spanish Sweetheart!" I cried. "The million-dollar dog!"

"That's right," Mrs. Nelson said. "Have you heard of her?"

"She is one of the basset hounds who disappeared," I said. "She has been missing since yesterday afternoon."

Mrs. Nelson gasped. "She must have vanished right after her owner dropped off the puppies."

"Don't worry. We're going to find Sweetie and all the other bassets," I told her. "But first we have to find 787 Treadmill Lane."

"Let me get you that map," Mrs. Nelson said. "You two have a seat on the couch. I'll be right back."

"Adios," I called after her.

I started toward the couch. Ashley grabbed me by the arm.

"Mary-Kate! I just realized why the curly-haired woman drove off so fast," Ashley said. "She was looking for Spanish Sweetheart!"

"Huh? I don't get it," I told her.

"You didn't want Clue to get too close to

the curly-haired woman, remember?" she asked.

I nodded. But I still didn't get it.

"You told Clue to sit—and she sat. Then the curly-haired woman jumped back in her van and drove off," Ashley explained. "Do you get it now?"

"No," I said. "I'm more confused than ever!"

"Spanish Sweetheart only understands Spanish. But you told Clue to sit in *English*," Ashley told me.

"I get it!" I snapped my fingers. "She figured out Clue couldn't be Sweetie, because Clue understood English."

"And as soon as she knew Clue *wasn't* the million-dollar dog, she wasn't interested in Clue anymore," Ashley pointed out.

"The curly-haired woman must be after the big reward," I said. "If she's the one who finds Sweetie, she'll be rich!"

Ashley and I slapped a high five.

"The nervous man could be after the

reward, too," Ashley reminded me. "He is still a suspect."

I nodded. "We don't know *who* the dognapper is yet," I agreed. "But at least we know *why* the dognapper is stealing the bassets."

"Right," Ashley said. "The dognapper is stealing all the bassets in town, hoping that *one* of them will turn out to be Spanish Sweetheart."

Mrs. Nelson hurried back into the living room. She unfolded a big map.

"There's an alphabetical list of streets," Ashley said. She ran her finger down the list. "Train Street. Treadmill Lane. Trotter Road."

Ashley gave a big sigh. "There is only one Treadmill Lane."

I sighed, too. Our great clue turned out to be useless.

"The nervous man gave a fake address," I said. "Now what do we do?"

Ashley didn't answer.

"What do you think we should do now,

Ashley?" I asked.

She didn't answer.

"What's wrong?" I asked.

"The puppies," Ashley said. "They are so quiet."

She was right. I didn't hear one puppy barking.

Ashley and I dashed to the back door. I jerked it open.

All six puppies were gone.

And so was Clue!

9

THREE DETECTIVES
ON THE CASE

"**H**ere, girl," Ashley called. "Come on, Clue."

But Clue didn't come.

I couldn't believe she was really gone.

"Cluuuuue!" I yelled. "Clue, Clue, Clue!"

I listened hard. I wanted to hear the jangle of Clue's collar. Or the sound of her paws on the driveway. But all I heard was a car door slamming. A car door!

"Let's go!" I shouted. "It could be the dognapper!"

I shoved open the gate and ran across the front yard.

I could hear Ashley a few steps behind me.

I stared down the street—and saw a flash of green turning the corner.

"It's the green van!" I yelled. "The one we saw the curly-haired woman driving!"

I dashed over to my bike and jumped on.

"Wait," Ashley called. "We need a plan."

"We have a plan!" I cried. "Follow that van and get Clue back!"

"Good plan!" Ashley hopped on her bike, and we started down the street.

I pumped hard on the pedals. I wasn't going to let the curly-haired woman have Clue!

I turned the corner.

I didn't see a green van anywhere.

"Oh, no!" I cried. "We lost her!"

Ashley and I stared at each other.

"How are we going to get Clue back—without Clue to help us?" Ashley wailed.

We had never tried to solve a case without

Clue before. But now we had no choice.

Maybe *I* should try sniffing the ground the way Clue did, I thought. My nose isn't nearly as good as hers. But maybe I would smell something….

I stared down at the ground—and saw a set of muddy tire tracks.

My heart started to pound. I stared down the street toward Mrs. Nelson's house.

Muddy tire tracks ran up her driveway.

"Follow those tracks!" I yelled. "I think the green van made them! There are some on Mrs. Nelson's driveway. And they turn the corner here—right where I saw the green van make a turn!"

Ashley and I flew down the street. At the next corner the tracks turned left. Ashley and I followed them, riding as fast as we could.

I spotted the green van almost two blocks down the street.

"Hurry!" I shouted. "She'll have to stop at that stop sign. We can catch her."

The van pulled up to the stop sign. A mother with a little boy holding her hand started across the street just in front of the van.

I pedaled even harder. My legs started to cramp. But I didn't stop. I couldn't. We had to get to the van before the mother and her little boy crossed the street! As soon as they crossed, the van would zoom away.

"Faster, faster, faster," Ashley chanted behind me.

We raced up to the green van.

The little boy tripped. The green van still couldn't move forward!

"Yes!" I cried. I jumped off my bike and pressed my face against the van's back window. Was Clue in there?

Ashley hurried up beside me. "Is she there? Do you see her?"

Bang!

A car door slammed.

The curly-haired woman marched up to me and Ashley. "What are you kids doing back there?" she demanded. She glared at us.

"Hey, I recognize you," she said. "You're the twins with the basset."

"We know who you are, too," I told her. "You're the dognapper who has been stealing all the bassets. You're trying to find Spanish Sweetheart so you can get the reward money."

"What did you do to our dog?" Ashley demanded. "Give her back to us—now!"

"I *am* looking for Spanish Sweetheart," the curly-haired woman said. "But I'm not a dognapper."

She smiled at us. "My name is Lydia Carver. I'm a private investigator. Sweetie's owner hired me to find her."

"We're detectives, too!" Ashley told her. "Two of our friends' basset hounds were stolen. Then we found out even more bassets have disappeared. And the dognapper just took ours!"

"The dognapper must think if he steals every basset in town one of them will have to be Sweetie," I explained.

"I'm impressed," Lydia said. "You two are really great detectives."

Lydia shook her head. "I don't know *what* happened to Sweetie. I thought maybe one of the other show-dog owners stole her—so Sweetie wouldn't win the big show tomorrow."

"There's one thing I can't figure out," Ashley said. "What were you doing at Mrs. Nelson's house?"

"I thought there was a possibility that Sweetie got out of her carrier on her own. Sometimes the owner's daughter forgets to make sure Sweetie's carrier door is shut," Lydia explained.

"I thought if Sweetie *did* get out, she might have gone to Mrs. Nelson's house to visit her puppies," Lydia continued. "When I pulled up to the house, I saw a truck driving away. A truck filled with bassets."

"Our dog Clue must be on that truck!" I exclaimed. "Where did it go?"

"I lost it," Lydia said. "While I waited for that mother and her little boy to cross the street, the truck got away."

"Too bad it didn't have muddy tires. That's how we caught you. We followed your tire tracks," Ashley said.

"But Lydia's tires aren't muddy!" I exclaimed. I pointed to her tires. There wasn't a speck of mud on them.

"That means the muddy tire tracks—" Ashley began.

"Belong to the dognapper's truck!" I finished.

"Let's go!" Lydia cried. "We have a dognapper to catch!"

10

201 BASSETS

Lydia climbed back in her van and followed the muddy tire tracks down the street.

Ashley and I followed Lydia. She drove slowly so we could keep up on our bikes.

We made a left turn, then a right turn. Then the tracks turned onto a dirt road.

"Uh-oh," I said. "We can't see the tracks anymore."

The muddy tracks didn't show up on the hard-packed dirt.

Lydia leaned out the van window. "I think

we should just follow this road and see where it goes," she called.

I bounced up and down as I pedaled over the bumpy road. I turned my head back and forth, searching for any sign of Clue.

The road made a sharp curve—and I saw an old house. The paint was peeling. Several windows were broken. Weeds grew through cracks on the porch.

"It looks like that house is abandoned," Ashley said.

"I don't see a truck," I added. "Do you think this is where the dognapper stopped?"

Lydia stopped the van and jumped out. "That house looks like a perfect hiding place," she said. "You two wait here, and I'll check it out."

Ashley shook her head. "We're on the case, too," she said.

"Yeah, we're going with you," I added.

"Okay, okay," Lydia said. "But we all have to be very quiet. If the dognapper *is* in there, we

don't want him to hear us."

We crept forward. My heart was pounding so hard I was afraid *it* was making too much noise.

"Listen," Ashley whispered. "Barking!"

We tiptoed over to the side of the house. The barking was much louder now. It sounded like a *lot* of dogs.

Lydia pointed toward the nearest set of windows. She took the one on the left. Ashley headed for the one on the right. I went to the one in the middle.

The window was a little too high for me to see in. I spotted a big rock a couple feet away. I shoved it under the window and climbed up.

The glass pane was cracked and grimy. I wiped a spot clean with my sleeve. I peered inside—and a big smile stretched across my face.

There were bassets inside. So many of them I couldn't count them all.

Bassets were snoozing on the dining room

chairs. Bassets were playing under the table. Bassets were eating and drinking from bowls lined up against a wall.

"Let's check the other rooms," Ashley whispered.

We made our way around the house and over to a big side window. We peeked inside.

My eyes widened. More bassets! The big living room was full of them!

A puppy ran up to the window and licked the glass. It had one brown ear and one white ear.

"Tim's puppy!" I exclaimed.

"Shh!" Lydia put her finger to her lips.

"Do you see Clue or Sparky?" Ashley whispered.

I stared around the living room. I saw all kinds of bassets. But no Clue, and no Sparky.

I shook my head. "We have to keep looking."

We rushed from window to window. There were bassets in the bedrooms. Bassets in the hallways. Bassets in the library. There were even bassets in the bathtub!

But no Clue.

"How many bassets do you think there are?" Ashley whispered. Even her super-logical brain couldn't keep track!

Lydia studied a small notebook. Maybe writing things down helped her think, too. Just like Ashley!

"There were twenty-four in the dining room," Lydia whispered. "Thirty-seven in the living room. Seven in the green bedroom. Eighteen in the yellow bedroom. Twenty-three in the blue bedroom. Twenty-two in the front hall. Eighteen in the den. Seven in the bath-room. And eleven here in the library."

"You counted them all? That's awesome!" I said. I tried to count them myself. But there were just too many of them—and they never stopped moving.

Lydia ran her pencil down the column of numbers. "That's one hundred and sixty-seven

basset hounds so far!"

"Wow!" Ashley exclaimed. She stared at Lydia. "Wow!" she repeated. "You're really an amazing detective."

"Not that amazing," Lydia answered. "I still haven't solved the case."

"There are two windows we haven't checked," Ashley said. She led the way to the back of the house.

I crossed my fingers. Clue and Sparky had to be here. They had to be.

Ashley and I pressed our faces against the closest window. We both gasped.

"Clue!" we exclaimed at the same time. Clue was in the kitchen!

Clue looked up. She has a great nose. But her ears are pretty good, too. She recognized our voices. She barked and ran over to the window.

Another basset followed her. Sparky!

Lydia was busy counting. "Thirty-four more," she announced. "That makes a grand total of…" She paused for a second while she added her column of numbers. "Two hundred and one dogs!"

"Two hundred and one bassets," Ashley corrected.

"Two hundred and one Clues!" I exclaimed. It sort of seemed that way. All the dogs looked a lot like Clue.

"We've got to get the bassets out of there before the dognapper comes back," I said.

Ashley tried the kitchen door. It wasn't locked. We dashed inside.

All the dogs started barking louder. Clue barked loudest of all.

Ashley and I both gave her a big hug.

"We found you!" I cried.

"Clue!" Ashley whispered. "I thought we'd never see you again."

I felt a cold nose press up against my arm. I looked down—and saw Sparky.

I gave his head a scratch. "Samantha is going to be so happy to see you," I told him.

I tried to hug Sparky and Clue at the same time. "We're going to give you two a big 'welcome home' party," I said. "With dog bones and—"

"What was that?" Ashley interrupted.

"A car door slamming! Someone must have driven up to the house!" I answered. My stomach flip-flopped.

"We've got to hide," Lydia said.

But it was too late.

The kitchen door flew open with a bang!

NOTHING BUT TROUBLE

A short man stumbled into the kitchen. He carried a huge bag of dog biscuits.

A clump of dog food was mashed into his thinning brown hair. The cuffs of his pants had chew-marks in them. He had pieces of cotton stuck in both ears.

He dropped the bag of dog biscuits on the floor. Three of the bassets rushed over and ripped it open.

"The nervous man!" I yelped.

"Larry Katz!" Ashley exclaimed.

"Huh? I can't hear you," he said.

Lydia marched up to him and pulled the cotton out of his ears.

"Too much barking," Larry mumbled.

"We know you stole these dogs!" I cried. "And you're giving them all back."

"Take them," he said. "Take them, please."

Larry gave a big sigh. "Do you know how hard it is to live with two hundred and one dogs? All the barking. All the drooling."

A puppy wandered over and started gnawing on Larry's shoe. "All the chewing," he added.

"Where is Spanish Sweetheart?" Lydia demanded.

Larry groaned. "She's not here."

"You dognapped two hundred and one bassets—and none of them is Sweetie?" Ashley cried.

Larry nodded. The clump of dog food fell out of his hair—and landed on his shoe. One of the bassets licked it off.

"I wanted to find the million-dollar dog," Larry said. "I wanted to get the big reward. But none of these is the right basset."

"Are you sure?" Lydia asked.

"I checked every dog for a heart-shaped birthmark. Every wiggling one of them," Larry said.

"Did you check their bellies?" Lydia asked. "That's where Sweetie's birthmark is."

Lydia picked up the closest basset and studied its stomach.

Larry groaned again. "I didn't think to check their stomachs," he admitted. "That would have saved me a lot of time."

"It would have saved you even more time if you'd known Sweetie is a grown-up dog, not a puppy," Lydia told him. She checked another basset's belly.

"I wish I had never heard of Spanish Sweetheart," Larry moaned. "All I want to do is get all these dogs back to their owners. And then I really want to apologize to each and

every one of them."

"You can start with us," Ashley said. She pointed to Clue. "This is our dog. And we were so worried about her!"

"I'm sorry," Larry Katz said. "I'm really, really sorry. I wish I hadn't made you worry. I wish I hadn't been so greedy. I wish I hadn't wanted that reward so much. It's caused me nothing but trouble."

I felt a tiny bit sorry for him. Taking care of one basset was a lot of work. I couldn't imagine taking care of two hundred and one.

"As soon as I finish checking the bassets for birthmarks, I'll help you return them to their owners," Lydia promised him.

"We'll help, too," Ashley volunteered. She checked the belly of the closest basset. "*After* we find Spanish Sweetheart."

"Right! This case isn't over until we find Sweetie!" I said.

12

202 CLUES

"**T**wo hundred and one dogs, and no Spanish Sweetheart. I can't believe it," I said.

Samantha's dad hurried into the backyard with another plate of his special walnut chocolate-chip cookies. He set them down right in front of Tim.

Samantha laughed. "My dad knows you too well, Tim," she said.

I took another sip of my lemonade. We were having a big "Welcome Back, Bassets" party in Samantha's backyard.

Lydia was there. And Clue and Sparky and Tim's new puppy were playing on the grass.

"At least you found Sparky," Samantha said.

"And Turkey," Tim added.

"Turkey?" I asked.

"That's what I'm going to call my puppy," Tim explained. "Did you see how fast he *gobbled* those doggy snacks?"

Samantha giggled. "I get it. You're calling him Turkey because he's such a *gobbler!*"

"Right," Tim said. "I'm so glad I own a dog now."

"You made a lot of other dog owners very happy today, too," Lydia said.

Ashley, Lydia, and I had returned every one of the two hundred and one bassets to their homes. Their owners *were* very happy.

But Lydia wasn't. I could tell she was thinking about Sweetie.

"Don't worry," I told her. "Olsen and Olsen will help you find Sweetie!"

"But she has her big show *tomorrow*."

Lydia sighed. "You'd better work fast."

Ashley pulled out her notebook and flipped it open. "Let's go over our clues one more time."

Clue wandered over to us, wagging her tail.

"Not you, Clue," Ashley said. "Clue*s*!"

Clue flopped down next to Lydia. She stuck her nose in Lydia's bag and sniffed at a bright yellow squeaky toy.

"That's Sweetie's," Lydia said. "I'm sure she wouldn't mind if you played with it, Clue."

But Clue jumped to her feet and loped over to the back gate. She gave a loud bark.

"Hey! I think the Super-Duper Snooper is on the trail of something!" Ashley cried. "Maybe Sweetie's toy gave her Sweetie's scent!"

Ashley and I leaped up and raced after Clue. Tim, Samantha, and Lydia raced after *us*.

I opened the gate for Clue. She trotted across the front yard and headed up Patty's driveway.

Clue stopped in the middle of the driveway

and started to sniff.

"That's where she lost Sparky's trail this afternoon," Tim said.

"Clue, it's okay." Samantha bent down and patted Clue on the head. "Sparky's home now."

Clue gave the driveway another big sniff. Then she scurried up to Patty's front door. She threw her head back and gave a long, long howl.

Another howl answered Clue. The howl came from *inside* Patty's house.

I pounded on Patty's door. Patty swung the door open—and a basset hound slipped out.

"Hey!" Patty yelled in surprise.

Lydia grabbed the basset and checked its belly. "Everyone, I want you to meet Spanish Sweetie!" she cried.

"Who is Spanish Sweetie?" Patty asked.

"The missing basset—who isn't missing anymore!" Ashley replied.

Ashley and I slapped a high five. "Case closed!" I shouted.

"Our silent partner did it again!" Ashley cried. "She found Clue number 202."

Tim and Samantha and Lydia gave a big cheer.

"I have to call Sweetie's owner right away," Lydia said. She pulled out her cellular phone and punched in some numbers.

Ashley stared at Patty. "You had Sweetie all along!" she exclaimed. "That's why you were asking all those questions about bassets at the mall."

"We've been looking for her all day," I added.

"You should have asked me," Patty said. "I found her roaming in my yard this morning."

"You know you have to give Sweetie back, right?" I asked Patty. I felt a teeny-tiny bit sorry for her. It would be hard to give up a great basset like Sweetie.

Patty tossed her ponytail over her shoulder. "Fine!" she exclaimed. "I don't want that dog anyway. She's really stupid. She doesn't do anything I say. Nothing!"

"That's because she only understands Spanish!" Ashley told her.

Patty opened her mouth. Then she shut it again. Then she slammed the door in our faces.

"Typical Princess Patty," Tim said.

Lydia folded up her cell phone. "Great news," she told us. "Sweetie's owner had two good ideas. Her first idea is that Larry should work at the animal shelter for free—to make up for worrying all the basset owners."

"That *is* a great idea," I said. "I know Larry will agree. What was her second idea?"

Ashley grinned. "She wants to give the reward money to the Olsen and Olsen Mystery Agency. She's so happy Sweetie is safe and sound."

"Why don't we give the money to the animal shelter?" Ashley suggested. "Then they can help more animals find good homes."

"Let's do it!" I exclaimed. Ashley's logical brain comes up with some great ideas.

"Sweetie's owner will love the idea of the reward going to an animal shelter," Lydia said. "I bet she'll even throw in some tickets to the dog show for all of you!"

"Cool!" Samantha exclaimed.

Lydia smiled at Ashley and me. "Thanks for all your help on the case. You two are doggone good detectives."

"This may have been our hardest case ever," Ashley said.

"It was pretty hard," I agreed. "But I'm not sure it was the hardest one of all."

"Of course it was," Ashley said. "Because we had to solve most of the mystery without our silent partner."

"That's right!" I exclaimed. "We solved the case without a Clue!"

Hi from both of us,

It's no secret that the Trenchcoat Twins love to solve mysteries. And we have even more brand-new mysteries for you to read! Mysteries that no one has ever seen or heard before—like the mystery we found at my horseback riding stable.

I love horses and riding. And I couldn't wait to ride my favorite horse—Hot Chocolate—in the next horse show. But somebody was trying to get me out of the show. No way! Ashley and I would jump over hurdles to solve *this* mystery!

Want to see how it all began? Take a look at the next page—and get a special sneak peek at The *New* Adventures of Mary-Kate & Ashley: The Case Of The Blue Ribbon Horse.

See you next time!

Love,

Ashley Olsen & Mary-Kate Olsen

"**M**y sister isn't a thief!" Ashley exclaimed.

Charlotte rolled her eyes in disbelief. "Then who is?" she asked.

"Maybe it's you," I said. "Maybe you're the one who rode my horse when you weren't supposed to. And maybe you left Hot Chocolate in a dirty stall in the barn!"

"Why would I do that?" Charlotte asked.

"To make me look bad," I replied. "And to keep me from riding in the big horse show."

"I don't care if you're in the show or not," Charlotte snapped back. "I'm a much better rider than you. And Magic is a much better horse than Hot Chocolate. You couldn't beat us—never, ever, ever!" Charlotte spun on her heel and stomped out of the stable.

I felt Ashley pat my shoulder. "Don't let her upset you, Mary-Kate," she said.

"I won't," I promised. "Because this is all Charlotte's fault. I know it. And I'm going to prove it!"

"Actually, you don't know it," Ashley told me. "It could be that somebody else is getting you into trouble."

I frowned. "Are you saying it *isn't* Charlotte's fault?"

"I'm saying that this is a mystery," Ashley declared. "We have to keep an open mind until we have all the facts."

"I guess you're right," I grumbled. But the horse show was only five days away. We had a lot of work to do if we were going to catch the culprit by then. Or else Hot Chocolate and I would never get the chance to win our first blue ribbon!

~The New Adventures of~
MARY·KATE & ASHLEY

NEW YORK CITY
BALLET SWEEPSTAKES

**You can win a trip to New York
City to meet Mary-Kate and Ashley
and see the famous New York City
Ballet perform George Balanchine's**
*The Nutcracker*SM**!**

Complete this entry form and send to:
The New Adventures of Mary-Kate & Ashley™
New York City Ballet Sweepstakes
c/o Scholastic Inc.
P.O. Box 7500
Jefferson City, MO 65102-7500

The New Adventures of Mary-Kate & Ashley™
NEW YORK CITY BALLET SWEEPSTAKES

Name_____
(please print)

Address_____

City_____ State_____ Zip_____

Phone Number (_____) _____
(area code)

Age_____

The New Adventures of Mary-Kate & Ashley™ New York City Ballet Sweepstakes

OFFICIAL RULES:

1. No purchase necessary.

2. To enter complete the official entry form or hand print your name, address, and phone number along with the words "The New Adventures of Mary-Kate & Ashley™ New York City Ballet Sweepstakes" on a 3 x 5 card and mail to: The New Adventures of Mary-Kate & Ashley™ New York City Ballet Sweepstakes, c/o Scholastic Inc., P.O. Box 7500, Jefferson City, MO 65102-7500, postmarked no later than April 30, 1998. Enter as often as you wish, but each entry must be mailed separately. One entry per envelope. Partially completed, illegible or mechanically reproduced entries will not be accepted. Sponsors are not responsible for lost, late, mutilated, illegible, stolen, postage due, incomplete or misdirected entries. All entries become the property of Scholastic Inc. and will not be returned.

3. Sweepstakes open to all legal residents of the United States, who are between the ages of five and twelve by April 30, 1998 excluding employees and immediate family members of Scholastic Inc., Parachute Properties and Parachute Press, Inc., and their respective subsidiaries and affiliates, officers, directors, shareholders, employees, agents, attorneys and other representatives (individually and collectively, "Parachute"), Warner Vision Entertainment, Dualstar Entertainment Group, Inc. and its subsidiaries and affiliates, officers, directors, shareholders, employees, agents, attorneys and other representatives (individually and collectively "Dualstar"), and their respective parent companies, affiliates, subsidiaries, advertising, promotion and fulfillment agencies, and the persons with whom each of the above are domiciled. Offer void where prohibited or restricted.

4. Odds of winning depend on total number of entries received. All prizes will be awarded. Winners will be randomly drawn on or about May 5, 1998 by Scholastic Inc., whose decisions are final. Potential winners will be notified by mail and potential winners and traveling companions will be required to sign and return an affidavit of eligibility and release of liability within 14 days of notification. Prizes won by minors will be awarded to parent or legal guardian who must sign and return all required legal documents. By acceptance of their prize, winners and traveling companions consent to the use of their names, photographs, likeness, and personal information by Scholastic Inc., Parachute, Dualstar, New York City Ballet and for publicity purposes without further compensation except where prohibited.

5. One (1) Grand Prize Winner will receive a trip for four to the New York City Ballet to see George Balanchine's *The Nutcracker*℠. Trip consists of round-trip coach air transportation for four people from the major airport nearest winner's home; hotel accommodations for two (2) nights (two rooms or a quad room); and four (4) complimentary seats at the New York City Ballet, as well as a pre-event back-stage tour and party with Mary-Kate & Ashley during intermission (Total approximate value: $3,938). Five (5) first prize winners will receive a New York City Ballet Nutcracker sports jacket (Total approximate value: $170 each); Fifteen (15) second prize winners will receive a Nutcracker doll (Total approximate value: $80 each); and Twenty-five (25) third prize winners will receive a New York City Ballet Nutcracker mug (Total approximate value: $12 each). Accommodations for the grand prize are room and tax only. Grand prize winner and traveling companions are responsible for all incidentals and all other charges, except hotel tax, including without limitations meals, gratuities, all taxes and transfers. Dualstar, Parachute, and Scholastic Inc. reserve the right to substitute another prize if winner is unable to attend on the specified date.

6. Only one prize will be awarded per individual, family, or household. Prizes are non-transferable and cannot be sold or redeemed for cash. Please allow up to seven weeks for delivery of first, second, and third prizes. No cash substitute is available. Any federal, state or local taxes are the responsibility of the winner.

7. Additional terms: By participating, entrants agree a) to the official rules and decisions of the judges which will be final in all respects; and b) to release, discharge and hold harmless Scholastic Inc., Parachute, Dualstar, New York City Ballet and their affiliates, subsidiaries and advertising and promotion agencies from and against any and all liability or damages associated with acceptance, use or misuse of any prize received in this sweepstakes.

8. To obtain the name of the winners, please send your request and a self-addressed stamped envelope (excluding residents of Vermont and Washington) to The New Adventures of Mary-Kate & Ashley™ New York City Ballet Sweepstakes, c/o Scholastic Inc., P.O. Box 7500, Jefferson City, MO 65102-7500.

Mary Kate & Ashley
Ready for Fun and Adventure? Read All Our Books!

The Adventures of MARY-KATE & ASHLEY™

Look for the best-selling detective home video episodes.

The Case Of The Volcano Adventure™	53336-3
The Case Of The U.S. Navy Mystery™	53337-3
The Case Of The Hotel Who•Done•It™	53328-3
The Case Of The Shark Encounter™	53320-3
The Case Of The U.S. Space Camp® Mission™	53321-3
The Case Of The Fun House Mystery™	53306-3
The Case Of The Christmas Caper™	53305-3
The Case Of The Sea World® Adventure™	53301-3
The Case Of The Mystery Cruise™	53302-3
The Case Of The Logical i Ranch™	53303-3
The Case Of Thorn Mansion™	53300-3

YOU'RE INVITED TO MARY-KATE & ASHLEY'S™

Join the fun!

You're Invited To Mary-Kate & Ashley's™ Birthday Party™	*NEW*	53355-3
You're Invited To Mary-Kate & Ashley's™ Christmas Party™	*NEW*	53356-3
You're Invited To Mary-Kate & Ashley's™ Sleepover Party™		53307-3
You're Invited To Mary-Kate & Ashley's™ Hawaiian Beach Party™		53329-3

And also available:

Mary-Kate and Ashley Olsen: Our Music Video™	*NEW*	53357-3
Mary-Kate and Ashley Olsen: Our First Video™		53304-3

DUALSTAR
VIDEO

KidVision
A DIVISION OF
WARNERVISION
ENTERTAINMENT

Listen To Us!

You're Invited to Mary-Kate & Ashley's™
Sleepover Party™
-Featuring 14 Great Songs-
Mary-Kate & Ashley's Newest Cassette and CD
Available Now Wherever Music is Sold

It doesn't matter if you live around the corner...
or around the world...
If you are a fan of Mary-Kate and Ashley Olsen,
you should be a member of

MARY-KATE + ASHLEY'S FUN CLUB™

Here's what you get:
Our Funzine™
An autographed color photo
Two black & white individual photos
A full size color poster
An official **Fun Club**™ membership card
A **Fun Club**™ school folder
Two special **Fun Club**™ surprises
A holiday card
Fun Club™ collectibles catalog
Plus a **Fun Club**™ box to keep everything in

To join Mary-Kate + Ashley's Fun Club™, fill out the form
below and send it along with

U.S. Residents – $17.00
Canadian Residents – $22 U.S. Funds
International Residents – $27 U.S. Funds

**MARY-KATE + ASHLEY'S FUN CLUB™
859 HOLLYWOOD WAY, SUITE 275
BURBANK, CA 91505**

NAME:_____

ADDRESS:_____

CITY:_____STATE:_____ZIP:_____

PHONE: (____) _____BIRTHDATE:_____